P9-CMX-590

and the Forest Friends

by **ANDREW STARK** illustrated by **EMILY FAITH JOHNSON**

PICTURE WINDOW BOOKS
a capstone imprint

Published by Picture Window Books, an imprint of Capstone.
1710 Roe Crest Drive, North Mankato, Minnesota 56003
capstonepub.com

Library of Congress Cataloging-in-Publication Data

Names: Stark, Andrew (Ojibwa Indian), author. | Johnson, Emily Faith, illustrator.
Title: Liam and the forest friends / by Andrew Stark;
illustrated by Emily Faith Johnson.
Description: North Mankato, Minnesota : Picture Window Books, an imprint of Capstone [2023] | Series: Liam Kingbird's kingdom | Audience: Ages 5-7. | Audience: Grades K-1. | Summary: Sometimes Liam, an Ojibwa boy, has to retreat to his room and escape into his imaginary world with the animal friends he has drawn, who can reassure him that whatever happens he is safe and loved.
Identifiers: LCCN 2022041484 (print) | LCCN 2022041485 (ebook) |
ISBN 9781666395075 (hardcover) | ISBN 9781484670637 (paperback) |
ISBN 9781484670644 (pdf) | ISBN 9781484683316 (kindle edition)
Subjects: LCSH: Ojibwa Indians—Juvenile fiction. | Imaginary companions—Juvenile fiction. | Life change events—Juvenile fiction. | Imagination—Juvenile fiction. | Friendship—Juvenile fiction. | CYAC: Ojibwa Indians—Fiction. | Imaginary playmates—Fiction. | Stress (Psychology)—Fiction. | Imagination—Fiction. | Friendship—Fiction. | LCGFT: Fiction.
Classification: LCC PZ7.1.S73758 Li 2023 (print) | LCC PZ7.1.S73758 (ebook) |
DDC 813.6 [Fic]—dc23/eng/20220830
LC record available at https://lccn.loc.gov/2022041484
LC ebook record available at https://lccn.loc.gov/2022041485

Designer:
Tracy Davies

Design Elements:
Shutterstock: Daria Dyk, Oksancia, Rainer Lesniewski

Printed and bound in the USA. 5195

Table of Contents

MEET LIAM KINGBIRD!

Liam loves to draw!

Liam is Ojibwa.

Liam is a good thinker.

Liam speaks two languages.

Liam likes animals.

WHAT MAKES YOU SPECIAL?

Chapter 1

RAIN

Whenever it rained, Liam liked to sit in his bedroom and draw stories. Outside his window, he had a clear view of the forest. It was lush and green on this spring afternoon.

Most of the stories Liam drew were about animals. He felt like he understood animals better than he understood people.

What do animals do when it rains? he wondered. How do they stay dry? He hoped their fur or feathers kept them warm.

Liam started to draw a great big bear.

First he drew the curve of the bear's huge head. Then he drew two fuzzy ears. Next he drew the bear's giant belly.

Liam smiled.

He didn't want Mr. Bear to be alone, so he started to draw another animal. He sketched the long neck of Ms. Giraffe. She was tall and thin, with long eyelashes. Mr. Bear was shorter and heavier. Liam gave him big claws.

Starting down by Ms. Giraffe's knees, Liam drew a little lion.

There, Liam thought. Now it's a family.

Chapter 2

INTO THE FOREST

As Liam drew, a story began in his head. In the story, the sun was shining. It never rained in Liam's stories.

The animal family came upon a field of wildflowers. This was Little Lion's favorite spot in the whole forest.

Just then, a butterfly bopped him on the head and fluttered past. Little Lion joined in a game of tag.

Mr. Bear sat with Ms. Giraffe. He seemed kind of grumpy.

"Do you like it here?" Ms. Giraffe asked Mr. Bear.

Mr. Bear looked around and shrugged. "It's just like any other forest," he said.

“But this one is special,” said Ms. Giraffe.

Mr. Bear asked, “What makes it so special?”

Ms. Giraffe bent way down to smell some flowers. “Because we’re here together,” she said.

Mr. Bear looked down to think for awhile. Ms. Giraffe watched him.

When Mr. Bear looked up, the grumpiness on his face had been replaced by something that Liam understood. But Liam didn't know what to call it.

Little Lion returned from his game. He curled up beside Mr. Bear and purred.

Mr. Bear patted him gently with his huge paw. "There's something we need to talk about," he said.

Chapter 3

ALWAYS FAMILY

"Ms. Giraffe and I are very different," Mr. Bear said. "I spend my days hunting for food, by myself."

"How else are you different?" asked Little Lion.

"Well . . ." Mr. Bear said, holding up his paw. "I have these really long claws."

“And I have this really long neck,” said Ms. Giraffe.

Then she reached high above them to nibble some leaves, just to make Little Lion smile.

"I sleep all winter long," said Mr. Bear. He shut his eyes and made loud snoring sounds.

"And I don't," said Ms. Giraffe. She slowly blinked her long eyelashes.

Then Mr. Bear said, "Ms. Giraffe can take very good care of you."

Ms. Giraffe bent way down again. She nuzzled Little Lion's face with her own.

"I'll be going to live in a different forest," said Mr. Bear. "One far away from here."

The little lion frowned. "How come?"

Ms. Giraffe said, "Because it's time to part ways. You and I will stay here, Little Lion. We'll stay in this special forest with your favorite meadow."

"Will we still be a family?" Little Lion asked.

Mr. Bear said, "We will always be a family."

"But when will I see you?" asked Little Lion.

"All the time!" Mr. Bear said. "Just look up at the stars every night, and there I'll be. I'm the biggest constellation in the whole sky."

Little Lion asked, "But what if it's cloudy and I can't see the stars?"

"I'll still be there," Mr. Bear said, "even if you can't see me."

Liam stopped drawing and stared out the window for a few moments. The rain had ended. It wasn't quite nighttime yet, but Liam looked up anyway.

FACTS ABOUT OJIBWA

WHAT'S IN A NAME?

The Ojibwa are Indigenous people also known as Ojibwe, Chippewa, Anishinaabe, and Salteaux, depending on where they live. Many live in southern Canada and in the northern Midwest and the northern Plains of the United States.

"BOOZHOO! HELLO!"

The Ojibwa speak an Algonquian language called Anishinaabemowin or Ojibwemowin, which are dialects that change slightly from region to region. Dialect includes word pronunciation, grammar, and vocabulary. Most speakers of Ojibwemowin live in parts of Michigan, Wisconsin, Minnesota, or southern Canada. A school in Wisconsin is called the Waadookodaading Ojibwe Language Immersion School. All of its classes are taught in the Ojibwa language.

A LONG, LONG TIME AGO . . .

The earliest Ojibwa stories were either handed down through oral histories or birch bark scrolls. These stories tell of the five original Ojibwa clans, or doodem. These were the Bullhead Fish (Wawaazisii), Crane (Baswenaazhi), Pintail Duck (Aan'aawenh), Bear (Nooke), and Little Moose (Moozoonsii). There was a sixth doodem, the Thunderbird (Animikii), but he was too powerful and had to return to the ocean.

WHAT'S FOR DINNER?

Today the Ojibwa live very much like many other Americans and Canadians and eat what they do. But the original Ojibwa people were hunters and gatherers. They survived on wild rice and corn, lots of fish, and small game like squirrels and rabbits.

OJIBWA KIDS: JUST LIKE YOU

In the past, Ojibwa kids played with handmade dolls and toys. Lacrosse was a popular sport among older children. Today Ojibwa kids go to school, play sports and video games, and hang out with their friends. However, many are still very connected to the outdoors and love to go hunting and fishing.

GLOSSARY

cleft lip (KLEFT LIP)—a condition in which the lip does not fully form before birth, resulting in a gap or opening in the lip; surgery can close the gap and may leave a small scar on the upper lip

constellation (CON-stuh-LAY-shun)—a group of stars

eyelash (I-lash)—the long hairs on the upper and lower eyelids that protect the eyes

lush (LUSH)—healthy and plentiful, especially in plant life

nuzzle (NUZZ-uhl)—to rub faces together to show care

sketch (SKETCH)—to draw lightly

wildflower (WILD-flouw-er)—a flower that grows naturally in an area

GIVE IT SOME THOUGHT

- In the story that Liam draws, Mr. Bear and Ms. Giraffe decide to separate. This worries Little Lion. Asking questions helps him to understand what is happening and how it might affect him. What other questions do you think Little Lion might want to ask?

- Divorce happens when a married couple decides to end their marriage and live apart. This change can be scary, especially when children are involved. Divorce is sometimes difficult, but it can also be a positive change for a family. It is important to understand that whatever the circumstances are, divorce is a personal decision between two adults.

- Doing creative things like drawing pictures, writing stories, or singing songs can help us understand our emotions. Can you think of a creative activity you like to do that helps you manage big thoughts or feelings?

ABOUT THE CREATORS

Andrew Stark was raised on the Ojibwa Indian Reservation in Michigan's Upper Peninsula. After earning his MFA from Pacific University, he moved to Los Angeles and began his career as an editor for a fashion magazine. He has since been published in a variety of publications, and one of his short stories was adapted into a stage play. He lives in Saint Paul, Minnesota, with his two dogs—Gizmo, a Chihuahua, and Barney, a chiweenie. Together, they love to camp and go hiking.

Emily Faith Johnson grew up on a farm in northern Wisconsin. She is a graphic designer, writer, and illustrator who loves bringing characters to life through her artwork. She's always secretly wanted to become a Broadway star, so when she's not writing or making art, you can usually find her serenading her goats and ponies with show tunes. She is a member of the Sault Ste. Marie Tribe of Chippewa Indians.